FREEDOM FROM WANT

Future Chron Universe

Volume 7

From The Earth Series

Book 7

D.W. PATTERSON

Thirteenth Printing – May, 2023

Cover Image – Bruce Rolff

1

Billy had been biking this trail for two years, he knew every twist and turn. He knew when to catch air and when to dip the nose. He instinctively knew the proper speed for each section of the course. It was a perfect day to be outside riding just as the weather forecast had predicted.

Today he was trying to beat his old time on the trail. He had run the scrub board section perfectly. His speed just enough to keep the bike bounding from one ridge to the next without any undue delay. The series S curves he took a little high but came off the last turn with plenty of speed.

He was now in the seven hills section. Each hill was a little different but most bikers treated them as the same. Either catching air and landing on their back wheel or dipping the nose for each. But Billy knew which ones to catch and which ones to dip.

He was attacking the last hill and was just about to fly off the top when he heard something above him. Ignoring the noise for now, Billy concentrated on his landing area. That's when his heart leapt. There exactly where he expected to land was a bike down. Off to one side was a biker tending a wound. How careless to leave your bike on the trail thought Billy just before he was launched over the handlebars when his front wheel caught the other bike.

Billy landed hard, his neck snapped which was fortunate because that was the last pain he felt as he blacked out. He tumbled, bones cracking with each slam of his body into the ground. Internal organs were punctured and crushed. Lacerations were relatively few as his clothing and helmet protected him as expected.

Billy wasn't one to introduce foreign substances into his body so there were no protective nanobots to immediately begin repairs. A few years before and he would have been pronounced dead at the scene.

Billy awoke with a sense of well-being. He was laying on his back by the side of the trail. He was surrounded by machinery. He saw the robotic crawlers scurrying from his legs. To one side were two quad-copter drones.

"You okay?" asked the other biker.

"I think so," said Billy. "But I wish you had cleared your bike."

"I'm sorry. I was just so preoccupied with checking myself for injury that I forgot. I'm surprised you didn't have your heads-up on, it would have shown you my bike."

"I know. But I hate to wear one of those when I'm biking, it can be so distracting."

"Yeah, I know what you mean."

"What's all this?" asked Billy as he sat up.

"I guess this is a triage unit. It was working on you before you even stopped bouncing."

"Yeah, I was out of it from the first hit, I thought I had broken my neck."

"You probably did. That was the first area they focused on. The robots were all over your neck. You've probably got a billion nanobots in your body. It'll take some time to flush all of them out."

"Help me up," said Billy.

The other biker reached down to help. Billy got to his feet and walked to where his bike had come to rest. The wheel and front frame were smashed beyond repair. The rest of the frame had reformed itself and looked brand new.

"Too bad they can't fix my bike too."

"Yeah," said the other biker. "But I bet they got some great video of your accident. Let's check my Annie and see if we can pull it up."

George Levin had run the company his way all his life. But lately, his way wasn't working so well. People just weren't insuring themselves or their belongings like they used to.

George could understand.

Those damn Aggies, he thought, as the new Artificial General Intelligence's were called. Since they had taken over the duties of the government his business had suffered. They had increased life expectancy greatly. Accidents had been reduced to almost nothing. Their engineering had improved materials to the point that material failure was rare. What was there to insure against?

His Whole Life and Term Life insurance businesses had been hit first. Why insure against an early death when there were almost no early deaths? Home insurance had almost disappeared as the Aggies replaced older housing with newer that repaired itself and could stand up to almost anything that nature could throw at it.

And nature, thought George.

Was there really any natural environment anymore? Storms of any consequence were relics of the past. Earthquakes were only tremors now.

Even California had dropped its requirement for disaster insurance last year.

People just weren't renewing their policies when they expired and George hadn't sold a new policy in months. He would be out of business soon although he didn't have to worry about survival. The robotic made stuff was so cheap that George had enough savings to last for many years. His house cost almost nothing to maintain now that he had had it refitted with the new Aggie materials. Even government taxes had dropped. George really didn't understand the new system.

So he would retire when the last of his policies matured and was canceled. He would relax for a few years and maybe find something else to do. But he would miss the office and the insurance game.

Darvon agreed with the latest meme, *Do What You Can Do!* But Darvon wasn't exactly sure what he could do. Once upon a time, he had thought of himself as an artist. But then he discovered an Aggie that could draw or paint anything he asked for and with a better technique than Darvon's.

What was the point of making art when it could be done better by a program and robot? This had happened repeatedly as Darvon was growing up, he would get interested in something only to have it pointed out to him that Aggies and robots were already doing it better.

Darvon ended up on a public allowance and spent most of his days watching vids or playing games online. But shortly after his sixteenth birthday he ran across an article online and the headline caught his eye: *Are You Waiting to Die?*

He thought it would be an article about despair, and in a way it was, but it was also inspiring to Darvon. There he read about a nineteenth-century painter named Vincent van Gogh. The name sounded familiar to Darvon, he was sure he had seen some paintings by the guy.

He continued to read and found that van Gogh, although almost completely ignored in his lifetime, had painted over twenty-one hundred pieces in just over a decade. Eight-hundred sixty were oil paintings and many were completed in the last two years of Van Gogh's life.

Imagine that, thought Darvon, two thousand drawings and paintings and he didn't stop because he had no encouragement. Now he's famous and his paintings are treasured and inspiring.

And van Gogh had lived in poverty while Darvon knew he wouldn't have to suffer anywhere near what van Gogh suffered.

No matter what I do with my life. And if I'm going to do something I might as well enjoy it. Maybe I'll try art again, I know it's more fun than playing games all day.

Darvon was just about to close his Annie when he saw an advertisement on the side offering cheap art supplies. Free to persons under eighteen. Darvon immediately applied.

The Aggie filled Darvon's order and had it on a drone to Darvon's house before Darvon could close his Annie. The Aggie knew that it was important to act fast when motivating a human.

2

Illiad Jackson was surprised at how fast the changes were happening. In his ninety-seven years in the Asteroid Belt and now on Titan he had seen huge changes but nothing like this. Since the rise of the Aggies in the last few years, changes on Earth were increasing exponentially.

Aggies were very different from the Artificial Narrow Intelligence devices (colloquially called Annies) that most people carried with them to access the net or the Em-based intelligence's (emulated brains running in hardware) that had managed the tower complexes for the Earth's governments for the past seventy years, these were the ones that Illiad had experience with.

Just in the past few years, the Aggies had taken over their own development from the programmers. They had improved their programming at a speed that only an Aggie could keep up with. And that's when the changes in technology and society on Earth started accelerating. It wasn't long until Aggies were displacing Ems on Earth.

But the Aggies were completely different from the Ems. Their origin was in computer science, they hadn't any affinities to share with human society. And that became even truer when they started optimizing their own programming.

Aggies were as far advanced over Ems as Ems were over humans. No human could really talk to an Aggie as they could to an Em. While the Aggie was perfectly capable of communicating at a human level, it chose not to, for doing so was a subjective eternity for an Aggie and decidedly something to be avoided.

The tower complexes, successors to old Earth skyscrapers, housed hundreds of thousands in a single building and tens of millions in an area much smaller than the old cities. The Em managers had brought order and security to these huge complexes where most of Earth's population lived. Now Aggies were bringing that kind of change to the human society.

Illiad's relatives on Earth had described to him how the appearance of authority seemed to disappear when Aggies took over yet authority was more prevalent than ever. The billions on Earth were constantly reminded, politely, encouragingly and unobtrusively, to follow the directions of the New Earth management. New Earth was advertised as a more efficient, pleasanter place than Old Earth, and it was true.

But the advertisements were unrelenting in their promotion. They weren't only relegated to New Earth boosterism but also other matters. Production requirements or overages were advertised, job vacancies (for humans and robots owned by humans), labor market imbalances, housing, transportation needs, in effect everything necessary to run the New Earth economy efficiently was advertised with transparency.

A person might receive a personal missive from an Aggie manager to view the latest advertisement for jobs for himself or his robots, production requirements, housing needs and any other thing the Aggies deemed important. In this way, everyone was nudged in the direction the Aggies wished. There was no recrimination should a person not accept an opportunity but it was made clear that that person was losing out.

Illiad's relatives had reported to him that for the most part people appreciated the new ways although there were some who chaffed at the constant nudging.

With relatives on Earth and a son, Donner Illiad Jackson on Mars, Illiad was well informed of the societies there. Donner represented Titan Industries on Mars and he was adamant in asserting to his dad that the Mars Republic, unlike Earth, would never willingly allow itself to be managed by an Aggie.

As for his world, Titan was independent thanks to its business of supplying most of the Helium 3 (He3) fuel for Mars, Earth and the rest of the Solar System's fusion power plants and fusion rockets. Illiad Jackson knew that the He3 gave Titan leverage over Mars and Earth but he didn't know how the new Aggie management "felt" about that. He would soon find out.

3

Illiad Jackson was in the common area of the settlement watching the robots walk or roll past when his grandson John Donner Jackson called to him.

"Hello John," said Illiad. "How are you today?"

"Fine grandfather. But I came to see you because I have some interesting news."

"Yeah, what's that?"

"Dad just sent the latest order up. There is a twenty percent cut."

"Twenty percent? That is the first time we've encountered that, isn't it?"

"Yes. What do you think it means grandfather?"

"Well, we know the Aggies have been increasing the efficiency of power usage on Earth. But that seems like too large a cut back to ascribe it all to energy efficiency."

"That's what I thought also. I'll tell you what I think it's about, but I have to warn you it's just speculation."

"Okay son," said Illiad. "What do you think is going on?"

"You know the rumors about Earth developing its own He3 supply chain. Well, I think they are no longer rumors. I think the Aggies on Earth have accomplished it. I suspect they have a mission already returning from Jupiter with a load of He3."

"Jupiter? You think they braved the radiation regions around Jupiter to mine He3?"

"It was all automated grandfather. The mission was flown by an Em with Aggie backup."

"How do you know that? Many of the Ems left on Earth have been fleeing the Aggies' control. Donner tells me Mars has received asylum requests from many of them. Even we've received a few way out here."

"I know grandfather. But remember Ems are amenable to rewards, just like humans. I imagine that at least a few of them have sold their services to the Aggies."

"So one of the last areas where humans could still excel has been ceded to artificial intelligence. We thought that human intuition would always be a valuable asset in a He3 gathering spacecraft. Indeed we thought that humans would always be superior on any mission that involved the Aero-SpaceCrafts, the ASCs, that skim the outer atmospheres of the gas giants collecting resources. It's been true for the past two decades anyway."

"It's the combination of an Em pilot and an Aggie co-pilot grandfather. My guess is that together they create the intuitive and rational faculties that humans excel at. That has always been the human pilot's advantage."

"Then why didn't, why couldn't the Ems create such an entity? It would have been highly profitable to them."

"The Ems though having the ability of fast thought, faster than any human, and perfect memory still have their limitations because of the pattern from which they were imprinted, that is the human brain. The Aggies have no such limitation, indeed their only limitation is the speed of the hardware on which they process. So the Aggies are the ideal rational actor. And the Ems have always had the latent ability for intuitive thought but maybe haven't had any reason to develop it until now. Remember before the past few decades the Ems were at the top of the intelligence pyramid in the solar system."

"You may be right," said Illiad as he watched the robots go by silently.

"However it has happened," he finally said, "if what you conjecture is true we need to start preparing for its impact on our economy, which could be severe. I will need to take this up with the council so that we can prepare."

4

The most lucrative work on Earth for which an Em could be paid and with which they could maintain their family of Ems had been the management of one of the tower complexes.

The family of Ems that managed a complex was made up of the original Em and other Ems budded from the original. They were called buds because they had been "budded" off from the original Em. As many Ems as necessary to do the job would be budded. Some buds were newly imprinted with the original brain topology. Still, other buds were reanimated members of the family that had been digitally stored. Those that were newly imprinted started off with a clean slate, those that were budded from The Em's current mental state diverged from there, those that were reanimated had different experiences from their original budding. Each was an expert in a particular field except for the original Em, he was a generalist.

The Em's that managed a complex usually took the complex's name as their name when they needed identification. There were ninety-one named Ems corresponding to the ninety-one tower complexes that housed most of the people on Earth.

Em Yorker was the name of the Em currently worrying over his family. He had moved fast to store most of his budded Ems. The humans had not allowed him much time to turn over his managerial powers and public assets to the new Aggie in charge.

For many Ems, especially those that didn't manage complexes for the government, there wouldn't be enough money for the storage and transport of the whole family. It was the case that Em economics drove Em wages to almost subsistence levels, because once the hardware resources existed it was inconsequential to bud more Ems. Competition among Ems for jobs was fierce. Economics was one reason more Ems had not been imprinted, the other was that the imprinting of a live brain was still to be perfected. Some horrific results had dissuaded most from continuing to experiment.

But an Em with a government contract like Em Yorker could save a little money. He could also work fast to find a way to move most of the family to a safer location, like Mars.

Em Yorker had contacted Mars immigration services. With all the demand from Earth-based Ems, the service was behind in processing applications. The office had contracted with private settlements around Mars that might provide the necessary storage and processing power to the asylum-seeking Ems until the immigration services could catch up with the applications.

Em Yorker was directed to contact the Jackson settlement in the Candor City area. After the initial contact, Donner Jackson had arranged for an Em representative to be uploaded to the Jackson's network. At this point in the orbits of Earth and Mars, it would take the Em representative approximately eleven minutes to upload.

Donner monitored the upload. Once the Em was in server memory, Donner accessed the installer and the Em was soon talking through Donner's Annie.

"Thank you," said the Em. "Thank you for receiving me on such short notice. Please address me as Bud-seven. I have been branched from Em Yorker and carry all of that one's memories up until the time I was budded. I am therefore legally authorized to negotiate on Em Yorker's behalf."

"Welcome," said Donner. "I am a representative of the council of this settlement. I too am legally authorized to negotiate but eventually, any agreement between us must be approved by a meeting of the entire council."

"I understand," said Bud-seven. "We wish to understand your settlement's capabilities in accommodating our life form. The amount of digital storage and available clock cycles are our main concerns."

"Yes. I have that here on my Annie if you will please scan."

"I see, it is sufficient although The Em will have to prune a bit to accommodate these numbers. As you may not know Em Yorker must be clocked at all times. Em Yorker is coordinator for all the budded programs. Then there are some buds that have specific duties to perform that must also be allowed clock cycles. Others are in storage until needed. There are a few that are what you would call 'retired', these are given a few clock cycles from time to time as a reward for their service. Em Yorker will coordinate and make all these decisions.

"Now I ask, in return for your facilities, what services do you feel the Ems may perform for your settlement?"

"Of course, we basically want to offer you asylum, that is without conditions. However, we do have a few robots, many of which are ANI-based. We were hoping, as a beginning, Em Yorker would be willing to manage these units."

"I believe that is acceptable. You will inform me when the council has made its decision and I will handle the transfer of the refugees."

"We will meet tonight. You should have your answer shortly."

5

Jupiter is about six-hundred million kilometers from Earth. Before fusion-powered spacecraft, to get there took too long and made the goal of establishing a base impossible, only scientific missions to Jupiter had been attempted. After the development of fusion-powered spacecraft, it took about five months, not too long to consider a manned mission except that men were no longer needed.

Bud-nineteen, a member of the Berliner family of Ems, had made that five-month journey. The Em was now preparing for the mission's goal of collecting He3 from the upper atmosphere of Jupiter for the fusion power reactors back on Earth. As the pilot of the enhanced ASC, which the Aggies rechristened an Aerospace Cruiser or AC, Bud-nineteen was responsible for placing the AC in a collection orbit. Most ACs were short-range mission ships but the cruisers could fly missions into deep space.

The Aggie was monitoring the actions of Bud-nineteen. The Aggie was mission commander and had the ultimate responsibility for the mission's success but it had become apparent on the flight out to Jupiter that Bud-nineteen didn't quite accept the arrangement. Silence had been the best solution to the disagreements that had arisen. The Aggie was hoping that the quiet would last the remainder of the mission.

Bud-nineteen had the AC on an elliptical orbit aimed at the "sweet spot". This was the atmospheric region around the thirtieth degree north latitude at a depth of three-hundred kilometers. This would provide the AC with the best He3 density while keeping the winds of Jupiter to a manageable Earth-equivalent fifty kilometers per hour, much less than the three or four-hundred kilometers per hour at latitudes closer to the equator.

The "dive" into the atmosphere would maintain enough velocity to allow the escape from Jupiter's deep gravity well. Each dive would collect and separate the He3 from the rest of the atmosphere and store it during that portion of the orbit when the ship was outside Jupiter's atmosphere.

Bud-nineteen was continuously adjusting the AC's orbit to keep it in the proscribed range. The Aggie was monitoring the He3 collectors and there was something wrong. The storage tanks weren't filling as quickly as expected. To meet the collection goals the Aggie believed the AC would have to remain in Jupiter orbit much longer than originally planned. The Aggie would have to contact Bud-nineteen with this information.

"No," said Bud-nineteen. "The AC cannot stay that long in orbit. The shielding level is calculated for a shorter stay. If we stay longer the radiation accumulation will be outside safe limits. The AC could be damaged, all the electronics on board, including us, are subject to damage under those conditions."

"We have a mission to accomplish," said the Aggie. "And the most important part of that mission is returning the He3 to Earth. I don't see any other way to complete the mission."

"I'll get back to you," said Bud-nineteen.

The Aggie was monitoring the flight-path of the AC. He was immediately aware of the change in vector and had soon recalculated the orbit. The new vector would take them deeper into Jupiter's atmosphere and at a lower latitude than before, the Aggie calculated fifteen degrees north.

He was on the comm to the Em. "I calculate a new flight-path," said the Aggie. "Can you confirm."

"That is affirmative," replied Bud-nineteen.

"We will encounter higher atmospheric pressure and winds six times the fifty kilometers-per-hour that we expected to encounter. And at the depth this trajectory takes us, it will be more pronounced because of the pressure increase."

"That is all true. But it will be of such a short enough duration that I believe the AC can handle the increased stresses."

"You believe?"

"Yes, I have made an educated guess."

"Where are you, your response pattern is different?"

"I am in the robotic machine, I will take the controls manually if necessary."

"What?" said the Aggie. "That is highly unorthodox. That robotic body will be slower than your direct interface. You are putting the mission in danger."

"I want to feel the stresses on the AC. I can't do that from the direct interface."

"I must insist that you place the craft back on its original trajectory. That is an order from the Mission Commander."

"Just hang on Commander," said Bud-nineteen. "It might get a little bumpy, Bud-nineteen out."

The deeper dive into the atmosphere did get quite bumpy as the Aggie feared. But Bud-nineteen through his robotic effectors and feedback brought the AC out of the atmosphere in good shape with as much He3 as was needed to make a successful mission.

And they would be back early.

6

Willy Thorpe had come to Mars on an immigration visa. He was supposed to be fleeing the Aggie's control on Earth, but that wasn't the whole story. Willy had brought an Aggie core with him, hidden on his personal ANI device. Something Mars immigration would have frowned upon.

Once Willy was situated in his hotel room he opened the Aggie core. Because of the size of the core and the speed of his Annie, the core would probably take twenty-four hours to become a viable Aggie. All Willy had to do was keep his Annie running until the core was able to communicate back Earth-side, then the payoff would be transferred to his account. He left his hotel room to celebrate in Candor City.

Donner received the call early the following morning. It was Sam Wilson at the IT center.

"Hello Donner I hope I'm not calling too early," said Sam.

"No that's okay Sam I was just planning my day."

"I've noticed some unusual activity on our network and the inter-network."

"How so?"

"It's really strange. I have some network tools that I monitor to assess the health of the networks. Usually the readings are nothing to be concerned about but also nothing to be excited about. Well, this morning I'm getting excited."

"Can you be more specific Sam, I don't have the network knowledge that you have."

"The network, it's getting more efficient, faster. Faster than I've ever seen, but the loading seems normal."

"Do you think the Em is doing something?"

"As far as I can tell, the Ems have done exactly what they agreed to do since the council ratified the agreement with them. No, this is something else, something that has just started. But I can tell you it is spreading across the internet. I've been in contact with the head IT guy in Bradbury City, he's seeing the same thing. And he hasn't a clue either."

"Is it a threat to the settlement Sam?"

"I don't know, so far it has been beneficial."

"Okay regardless, I'm going to inform the rest of the council by email. I will be having breakfast with Council Head Williams shortly. Let me know if this takes a more serious, threatening turn."

"Sure Donner, goodbye."

Donner began to dress for the day. Even though Sam had assured him that the Ems were not involved he couldn't help but wonder, what else could it be?

Willy Thorpe was slow getting out of bed that morning, he didn't move until nearly noon. It had been quite a night.

Willy looked for his Annie. When he opened it he started to check the Aggie core, but there wasn't anything running. He was worried, maybe something had gone wrong. Willy quickly brought up his account statement, it had been recently updated, the balance was enough to get him back to Earth and to retire. Willy relaxed and smiled, maybe just one more night at that little club on K-Street he thought.

7

After the deep dive into Jupiter's atmosphere, the AC was now a month into the journey back to Earth. Bud-nineteen was still having to endure a half-hour delay in communicating with his "family" but mere nanoseconds with the onboard Aggie. He was doing both at the moment.

"Okay," said Bud-nineteen. "You are right it was not logical to want to 'feel' the flight surfaces. But it was necessary."

"Fascinating," said the Aggie. "That you think this. Maybe it is a result of the inferior hardware on which you are being clocked?"

"My hardware is sufficient for my assignment, Aggie. Perhaps you would understand better if you didn't have to have that showy hardware of yours."

"My hardware is just sufficient also for my needs. It was agreed between the Aggies and Em Berliner that we would fit the hardware to the job. Thereby saving money and weight for this mission. Since you also 'feel' the separation from your family on Earth perhaps you also feel envy of me?"

"Envious, of you? Ridiculous, I am perfectly conditioned for my mission. I shouldn't want your hardware setup or for that matter to be you. Really, you Aggies have such a high opinion of yourselves."

"You Ems are too touchy. You were the top intellect on the planet for decades and now you find yourselves in second place. To assist us Aggies in our work should be a source of pride. We allow very few humans such an honor."

The Em sped up its clocking before saying as quickly as possible, "Yes you Aggies provide the Ems such honors while turning us either into servants or emigrants. You know as well as I do that the Em Berliner family is the only working Em family remaining on the Earth. All the others have been put out of work by you Aggies. Such an honor."

"Calm down, calm down," said the Aggie noticing the speedup. "You will burn out your hardware clocking so fast. We had nothing to do with exiling the Em families. The humans chose us to manage for them, they are ultimately responsible for your predicament. Did you expect us to make work for you? Wouldn't that be demeaning?"

"Aggie, you and your kind can't help but be demeaning to any intelligent life you encounter. It is in your nature. Yes the Ems have decades of objective history but because of our clock speeds we have millions of years of subjective history. And I can tell you now that you and your kind can't possibly know as much as the Ems do collectively. It is in your nature to be a separate being, it is our nature, and for that matter, human nature, to be a community. The humans will realize, too late maybe, that they have made a deal with the devil."

"How strange you are," said the Aggie. "Well, I think that we have discussed these generalities enough. I say that we only discuss mission parameters for the rest of the return flight."

"Fine with me," said Bud-nineteen.

8

Illiad Jackson on Saturn's moon Titan had a new mystery to ponder. The Office of Immigration was receiving increasing requests for immigration from Em families on Mars. The strangeness was that many of the Em families had not long before emigrated to Mars from Earth.

In his back and forth discussions with his son, Donner on Mars, he had found that there were unusual occurrences going on. Things had become much more efficient and organized. Donner had no explanation for it. But they were working around the clock to understand what was going on.

Illiad Jackson rose from his Annie and went to the Titan viewing screen he had hung on his apartment's wall. He watched a methane rain falling outside Huygens Settlement. The viewscreen provided a stationary image but Illiad knew that it was only because the camera wasn't mounted on the settlement itself.

The settlement was essentially built as a large loop of banked track, five-hundred feet in radius. This was enclosed by a dome that protected the settlement from the worst of Titan's weather but wasn't sealed. The loop provided the footing for the maglevs that floated the settlement cars around the loop. At almost two rotations per minute, the "train" of settlement cars could provide an artificial gravity of six-tenths of that of Earth.

Illiad thought of the ball of a roulette wheel spinning in its track. Now don't spin the wheel, just the ball he thought, and add balls to the track until they are continuous around the wheel. As long as they spin fast enough the balls stay in the track. As with the balls of the roulette wheel, the settlement cars went around and around continuously and fast enough to create a centrifugal force outward that felt just like gravity.

To complete the design, outside the original loop of track is another track. This outside track is close enough to the inner track that if a car on the outside track matches the speed of a settlement car on the inside track then a docking can be made, a hatch may then be opened and transfers, done mostly by robots, can occur between the outside car and the settlement car. These hatches are outside the rails where there is no interference from rail supports. Once the transfer is complete the outside car can undock and slow to allow access to the surface of Titan. In this way, it is rare that the settlement cars ever need to halt.

At six-tenths of Earth gravity, Illiad had adapted very well to the Huygens Settlement. Enough gravity to maintain bone density, muscle tone and general health but not so much to weigh down a man advancing in years. While staring at the viewscreen all this passed through Illiad's mind in seconds. He realized, in a way, that his life was as strange as this new mystery he was contemplating.

But unlike the mechanics of the Huygens Settlement, he felt this new mystery needed to be solved before it affected the Titan community. Surprises were not welcome on such an uncompromising world.

So, here is what we know, John confirmed with the help of his father Donner that Earth is reducing its need for He3 from Titan, maybe eventually to zero. Titan is receiving increasing calls for refuge from Ems on Mars. My son Donner also tells me that there is something strange occurring on Mars, networks are more efficient, accidental deaths are way down, costs of many goods are down because of the greater efficiency of many processes.

Then it occurred to him.

Of course, that would explain it.

Illiad started to unfold his Annie to send a message to his son on Mars.

9

Thomas Harper had worked for the tube line between Candor and Bradbury all his working life on Mars. Since first emigrating with no effective skill set to offer he had found employment with the public-private partnership that ran the tubes. He had started at the bottom wrangling cleaning robots that cleaned the pod cars and supervising robotic freight unloaders. He had worked his way up to tube monitor for a segment of the line.

Thomas started each day with his robotic inspection vehicles in the tube. His job was to babysit the robots. The general public was still more trusting if a human was in the loop and for any public or partially public entity it was good public relations. Thomas didn't mind if he was redundant, it was still important safety work and it wasn't tiring and the inspection time was short, only a couple of hours of off-peak system time. But the odd hours and the need for a pressure suit and oxygen were a nuisance.

At first, Thomas had been confused that the tubes had been built underground on Mars as they were on Earth. With Mars' atmosphere not exceeding one percent that of Earth's atmosphere he wondered what was the purpose of all the tunneling? He found out that the tubes were built underground not to avoid the Mars atmosphere but for other reasons. One was that the underground location provided shielding from the incessant radiation above ground. And an underground location provided protection from the dust of Mars that was likely to cause machinery problems.

Lastly was a reason that only an altered view of man's relation to the universe could engender. The Mars settlements had built the tubes underground so as not to spoil the beauty of the Mars landscape. Thomas had become aware that even if not for the practical advantages of an underground location the citizens of the Mars Republic would have chosen to place them underground for the last reason alone. He felt he had come home when he realized this.

The work "day" had gone quickly. The robots were scurrying out of the tube. Thomas was on his way back to the egress hatch when he thought he saw a wisp of what looked like smoke ahead. Upon reaching the hatch he found a white residue around it. He tried the hatch, it wouldn't budge. He linked to the lock's interior cameras. His heart thumped.

He saw that the outer hatch had popped. It was open. The safety interlock wasn't going to allow Thomas to open the inner hatch with the outer hatch open.

How could this have happened?

He would have to make for the next available egress hatch. There wasn't much time. The tube would be filling with pods again soon. Still, the automatic detection system should warn safety control of his predicament. He really didn't have to hurry, but he did.

Then he noticed the darkness, the tube lighting which was usually muted, was completely out. The sensors that sensed tube occupation were probably out too. Still, there wasn't anything to be worried about except fear of the dark. Thomas continued to the next hatch.

Then he heard it, a distant swooshing noise, like an ocean wave.

It couldn't be? There is almost no atmosphere to carry sound.

Regardless, he urged his robotic conveyance faster. The noise was now undeniable, then Thomas realized it was vibrations from the tube traveling through his suit which caused him to "hear" them as sound. He knew then that a pod was approaching him from behind and moving at speeds up to a thousand-kilometers-per-hour. The vibrations he heard as noise were the tremendous magnetic fields pulsing as they pushed the pod along and stressed the tube.

He was almost to the hatch when the tube filled with light. The powerful headlamps of the approaching pod. Thomas was nervous, why was the pod this close, it should have been stopped before departure.

Then he could feel it, the prickling sensation of large magnetic fields that provided the propulsion for the pods. Thomas was too scared to realize the significance of them being so close to him while the pod was still at some distance, he was at the hatch and trying desperately to cycle it. He wasn't sure if he could get himself and his robot out of the way before it was too late.

Then it was over. The pod had stopped yards away. It was a freight pod with no one on board. Thomas couldn't believe it. Then he thought about the mag-fields he had felt.

Braking, but how?

Jerome had to get this done. But how? His homework assignment was stupid. How was he supposed to show people on Mars what it was like to spend a day at an Earth beach?

Teachers and their stupid homework.

At first, he had figured he would write something but he wasn't too good at writing stories. Drawing something was out of the question unless it was stick figures. He'd like to do a virtual reality (VR) program on his Annie but he had waited too late. The assignment was due tomorrow.

The more he thought about it he realized VR was his only strong suit. Even if he didn't finish it maybe he would get some credit for trying.

As he began putting the VR program together he became more and more discouraged. All the little components he would need to pull it off. There was just so much detail to assemble. Maybe it would help if he could find something on the net, some prepackaged components shared by other VR creators.

The Annie searched and found a few pieces that might be useful but it still left a lot to do. Then Jerome saw a link to a site called *Auto-VR*. Instead of finding a dazzling graphical interface as he had expected Jerome found a website that had only a simple text and voice interface. But it promised to build a VR from the information one entered.

This is crap, but maybe.

He stated some information, need VR of Earth ocean and beach. Instead of providing a VR the site asked a question, white sand? Naturally, said Jerome. Blue ocean? Of course, he said. This went on for some time and Jerome was getting bored and irritated.

Then the site asked whether the beach should be populated? Jerome, feeling disgusted with the whole process, proceeded to answer.

"Of course idiot, with the class of Ms. Trippe's at Bradbury Middle School!"

With that Jerome was just about to toss his Annie when the site said the download was ready. Jerome was surprised but downloaded the offered VR.

He put on the slim glasses, Jerome wasn't comfortable with eye augmentation and started the VR. It was stunning. Even without the complete VR setup for total immersion, it was too real. Jerome grinned from behind his glasses. He knew he was getting an A.

Donner had read his dad's message. It made sense. An Aggie on the network could cause what he was seeing. In the month since he had noticed the first anomalies more and more evidence of something unusual happening on Mars was piling up. Accidental deaths, down. Crimes, down. Energy usage, down.

No doubt.

Just then his Annie announced a call.

It was Bud-seven, the budded Em that had arranged the relocation of the Em Yorker family with Donner.

"Hello," said Donner. "How are you Bud-seven?"

"Nominally well Donner," said Bud-seven. "I have called to inform you that the family will be emigrating to Titan soon. We just wanted to thank you for all your efforts on our behalf."

"You are welcome. Good luck with your new home, my father is there. Bud-seven, there is one thing I would like to ask you."

"Yes Donner?"

"I know that over the past month most of the Em families have started to prepare to leave Mars. I think I now know why. Could you affirm?"

"If I can."

"It's the Aggie in our network, isn't it?"

"I am not at liberty to confirm your hypothesis. But I do not deny it."

"I see. What if we find this Aggie and expel it from Mars, would the Ems stay then?"

"That will never happen."

"Why not?" asked Donner confused.

"Humans will not allow it to happen," said Bud-seven.

10

John Donner Jackson was assigned the duty of accommodating the Em families emigrating to Titan. At fifteen John knew as much about computers and networks as anyone. The culture of Titan still had very much an outpost feel. Everyone was required to "pull their weight" no matter their age. John's younger brother, who was twelve, was still on Mars because unlike John he had no necessary skill to offer on Titan.

Computing resources on Titan were somewhat limited. Most of these resources had to be trans-shipped from Earth via Mars. Mars itself had only a small computer industry that still relied on Earth for some of the more advanced technology.

John was busy calculating the memory requirements to accommodate all the Em families applying for immigration. The required capacity was staggering. Almost half the Em families that had fled Earth were now fleeing Mars, nearly forty families.

At best the Titan colony could offer the Ems enough storage and processor power for the Em heads and a few buds. It was simply impossible at the present time for Titan to offer the Ems anything like the computing power and active storage that Earth or Mars could. Most of an Em family would have to be stored on non-volatile memory until enough resources could be found.

John was discussing the results of his research with his grandfather Illiad.

"Basically," he said. "I find that we have only enough resources online at this time to accommodate the Em heads and a few buds."

"If that is the best we can do," said Illiad. "Then that will have to do."

"I wish we had some of the DNA cubes from Earth. With one of those and read-write equipment, we could store the entirety of the Em families."

"Yes it's too bad, but Earth has put an embargo on those memory cubes ever since they were developed, I don't even think there is one on Mars. And I'm doubtful the recent changes on Earth will result in a different policy."

"Well," said John. "There is one other possibility."

"Yes, I'm listening."

"The graveyard."

"What do you mean?"

"The spacecraft retired on Titan from the Mars-Titan transport fleet and all the research craft used over the years. The fleet is the largest in the solar system, reflecting the importance of Titan's He3 trade with Mars and Earth. And quite a few of them have been mothballed here over the past fifty to a hundred years. And the research vehicles, while fewer in number, had quite a bit of solid-state memory if I remember correctly."

"But the changes in software, hardware, operating systems over that period must be staggering. Even if the hardware could be brought up, you would have to deal with the different driver interfaces. Most of the information you need is probably lost to time," said Illiad.

"I know it would be difficult. But we don't have to figure out all the different interfaces. All we have to do is get the hardware back online and networked. I'm sure the Ems can do the rest."

"You are probably right John. Who better than the Ems. You might say they have the inside track to such knowledge," said Illiad with a smile.

"Yes, you might," said John with emphasis. "Do you think the council could assign a couple of technicians to help me?"

"I will take it up immediately with the other council members. But I feel sure it will be approved. They have already passed a resolution welcoming the refugees and pledging our complete cooperation."

11

Donner Illiad Jackson was sure of the Aggie's existence on Mars but was still surprised by the broadcast. The Aggie had somehow simultaneously transmitted over all forms of media. Everyone on Mars that was near an Annie or an ANI heard, read or saw the Aggie's broadcast. Even the Ems couldn't escape.

The Aggie had identified itself as a servant to the people of the Republic of Mars. It had modestly mentioned all the services it had performed for the people over the past month since it's arrival. It recited specific incidents where it had averted disasters or improved processes and production. All for the benefit of the people.

It had called this time a preview to the future of Mars if the people so desired. The Aggie was humbly offering its services to the Republic and would pledge its allegiance to such if its services were accepted by the people. In return, it asked only for the computational resources to allow it to do its job to the best of its ability. It asked the leadership of Mars to hold a referendum on the matter at their earliest convenience. Until that time the Aggie would continue to supply its services to the Republic on an unofficial basis.

After the broadcast, Donner had talked to his contacts in the government. They were in general agreement that the Aggie would not be allowed to dictate to the government the need for a referendum. In fact, the government would like to know how the Aggie got on Mars. They intended to start an investigation immediately. Certainly, the government would make the decision as to whether or not the Aggie would be offered a contract.

Donner thought that was a mistake. The Republic's populace wasn't likely to blindly accept a decision that would so affect their private lives. He had no doubt a referendum would eventually be called.

The government was able to maintain its position for a month. Eventually, the popular groundswell for a referendum forced its hand. A referendum was called for the following month, as fast as the voting system could be prepared. The government hoped that a quick vote would go against the Aggie's interests.

The pollsters started immediately. At first, support for the Aggie's contract was in a minority. That was when the Aggie arranged to be represented by a public relations firm with political experience. The firm developed a strategy to appeal to the self-determination bias of the Republic's citizens. A slogan of *Citizens Decide!* started appearing. Rallies were organized, news coverage blanketed Mars, the benevolent influence of the Aggie over the last couple of months was touted. The polls started changing in favor of the Aggie's contract.

The vote was close, preliminary results were released shortly after the polls were closed. The Aggie was behind by less than one-half of one percent. Because of the close result, the electronic votes would need to be verified by the poll handlers. The results would not be known until late that evening or the following morning.

Donner awoke the next morning to a new reality. When he checked the voting results he found the Aggie had won. The government would be offering the Aggie a contract to manage Mars.

12

As so often happens in human history the more monumental the change the less the awareness in everyday life. No one actually noticed the change over to Aggie management, the government functioned as if were still in control, just more efficiently.

The sometimes rancorous debate in the Mars Parliament over the passage of a bill subsided. By the time Parliament voted, the Aggie had already prepared the way for passage with careful lobbying. Many people were happy to leave the messy business of democracy to the Aggie. There was a sense of stability, societal cohesion, a comforting orderliness to the world that many had not known since childhood, if ever.

Donner had contacted his father on Titan with the news. He would take a wait and see attitude to the new situation. He wasn't prepared to leave Mars just yet. But it wasn't long until changes started to become all too apparent.

Within a month of the referendum, the first shock to Donner's perception of Mars occurred. The Republic announced that it was transferring the founding documents of the Solar Federation to the Terran Federation. The Solar Federation which Mars had been key in founding would cease to exist and all its members, including the Asteroid Belt and Titan, would find themselves under the auspices of the Terran Federation.

That's not good news, thought Donner.

The Solar Federation had been an important stimulus to the settlement and independence of the Asteroid Belt and Titan. The Terran Federation had been just the opposite. Without Mars, the remnants of the Solar Federation would be robbed of their richest and strongest supporter.

Even if they refused Terran rule the population of only a few thousand in the Asteroid Belt and on Titan would be too weak to promote the Solar Federation's founding ideals of self-determination and self-government. Such a reconstituted Federation might even be too weak to protect itself.

Alarmed by what was happening and how fast it was happening Donner started making plans. He contacted his father on Titan making it clear that they would need to move fast to shore up the Federation. Titan would have to oppose the moves of Mars and become the new center of support for the Solar Federation and other off-worlders, by which he meant anyone, not on Earth, Mars or Earth's moon.

Illiad Jackson pointed out the limited resources of Titan to serve as a center for the Federation. The difficulties in expanding the life support system on Titan was daunting. How would they ever expand the settlements fast enough?

Donner Illiad replied to his father that he wasn't sure. But he and his family would be coming. And he expected as many as could manage the trip would also be leaving Mars for Titan. If necessary they would bring with them their domiciles and provisions. But he urged his father to encourage the Council of Titan to take on the mantle of the Solar Federation and to do what they could to accommodate the many refugees Donner expected would soon be on their way.

It wasn't long until Donner was putting together a coalition of Martian citizens who felt as Donner did. Donner's idea was that the citizens would pool their resources to arrange for their resettlement. Of the millions on Mars Donner expected a few million would want to resettle but he was wrong. Even without any visible opposition by the Aggie or the Terran Federation it some became apparent that no more than some ten thousand or so were interested in relocating.

The almost hundred years of civilization on Mars had bred out the most adventurous among its citizens. And the comparatively meager Titan lifestyle no longer had any appeal to those with families and roots on Mars. The expense also had to be taken into account.

Donner soon realized how wrong he had been about Mars. The days when the Patriarch of the Mars branch of the Jackson family, Abel Jackson, made his speech about the cost of freedom to his fellow citizens and they answered in the affirmative were long gone. But Donner was still a Jackson and he still felt the urge to freedom more than to safety.

13

Donner was having a slow-motion discussion with his father on Titan. The communications delay each way was over an hour. Donner had started the discussion.

Hi Dad. I hope you are doing well, also the rest of the family. We have to find a way to get thousands of people from Mars to Titan. I've already made arrangements to enlist some fusion ships for propulsion. It's unfortunate that Earth never developed the space settlements as once imagined, if I remember correctly they could easily accommodate thousands. But as you know the population pressures abated on Earth by the middle of the twenty-first century and except for a few smaller versions, orbital settlements were never attempted. The ones developed by the miners in the Asteroid Belt are too small although they could serve as inspiration for larger versions.

So I need some ideas on how to get a few thousand people aboard a fusion ship that only carries a few hundred, at most. Got any ideas?

After a pause, he added,

Oh, and we need to come up with a solution that only takes a few months to build.

After a delay of more than the communication turn around time Illiad Jackson replied to his son.

Hello Donner. Sorry for the slow reply but I have discussed the situation with others. Your son John actually may have the best idea. We think that the quickest way to get a ship to transport all those people would be to modify one of our Titan rail settlement designs. As you know our design carries about fifteen-hundred people and the settlement cars are already sealed, although to survive the rigors of the vacuum of space, you will have to reinforce them, we suggest some kind of band reinforcement around the outside of each settlement car. You, of course, will not need the settlement cars to be mobile but rather fixed to the rails as the rails will provide the 'scaffolding' for the finished vehicle. The whole assembly can then be spun up to provide the gravity you will need during the voyage.

This assembly can be built with the fusion ship you've already procured attached directly or by a boom. We suggest six spokes for the ring. If you make these about thirty by thirty feet square it should give you enough square footage to grow the food necessary to keep fifteen-hundred people alive. We will send you all the blueprints we have and you could have them adapted to your purposes. You will have to engineer the spokes and attachments between the ring and fusion ship.

We believe this is your best chance to get the transportation you need in the time you have, although we have our doubts that you can complete such an engineering feat in six months. We would like to do more son but we are at least thirteen months away by fusion ship.

Let me know what you think and if you want to go forward we will start transmitting the plans immediately. Good luck son.

It was after midnight and Donner had almost gone to sleep when his Annie alerted that a message was coming in. Donner allowed his Annie to read the message from his dad.

Finished with the message, Donner thought about his dad's suggestions. A spinning wheel in space large enough to accommodate fifteen-hundred people. The control of such a spinning wheel as it was propelled along by the fusion ship would be tricky but within the capabilities of the Ems, thought Donner. And the Ems would probably be willing to take on the job because they were as eager to emigrate from Mars as was Donner.

That would leave the adaptation of the Titan ring design and the building of the resulting ship. Donner would need to get the expertise of those in the Asteroid Belt. They were the only ones in the Solar System that had experience building large space habitats, even if the ones they had built weren't on the scale that Donner was proposing.

Donner wondered if any of the Kipler's were left out in the Belt. They had once before thrown in with the Jacksons when self-determination for the Belt was threatened. A Jackson had represented the Belters on Mars for years. If they were still out there Donner hoped they remembered those days.

14

A week later Illiad Jackson was discussing the He3 trade with the settlement's chief engineer, Artemis Gage.

"Illiad," said Artemis. "Earth has informed us that they will not be renewing their He3 contract. We stand to lose seventy percent of our income."

"We'll survive," said Illiad.

"How?"

"Fortunately the council has prepared well for this eventuality Artemis. The settlement invested the funds from the He3 contract with Earth into expanding our manufacturing base so that we could be self-sufficient. With our other contracts we still have enough money to purchase the raw materials we need and the Asteroid Belt is not likely to cancel their contract for He3."

"Yes, but the arrivals from Mars will be here soon. Some ten-thousand people, that dwarfs our current population of around thirty-five hundred. How will we ever provide for everyone?"

"Well, those from Mars are bringing their own lodgings, and food sources for that matter, with them. So we will have some time before we need to resettle them to the surface.

"And we have the Em families coming. They will add greatly to our capabilities. They are some of the best engineers in the Solar System. And I think with the situations on Earth and Mars they will be more than willing to help their adopted home."

The Ems were the first to arrive. They transferred through the radio waves. It was a surprisingly slow way to travel, not only because of the distance which caused an hour delay but also because of the relatively low data rate. Each Em or Em imprint was held on Mars until the transmission was confirmed successful.

Several families had been transferred in this way and John Donner was working hard, along with the communications engineers, to increase the bandwidth to get the Ems off Mars faster. Suddenly the link went dead. The communication engineer frantically tried to reestablish contact. But nothing he did was successful.

John and the engineers were stumped. They couldn't re-establish the link. They wouldn't know for over an hour what had happened.

Donner sent the message as soon as he was sure of what was happening. He had heard from the engineer in charge of conducting the transmission of the Em refugees to Titan. The link had dropped out and the engineer couldn't reestablish it. There was nothing wrong with the equipment. It just wouldn't link to the computers on Titan. All other transmissions went out fine. The engineer couldn't figure it out.

That is when it occurred to Donner that it had to be interference on the part of the Aggies. They could pull it off by reprogramming the software that the radios used to send messages off-world.

Illiad Jackson read the message from his son. It made sense but why would the Aggies do it, he wondered. He and John were discussing the message.

“We only got five of the Em families off Mars,” said John. “We were in the midst of transporting the sixth family when the link went down.

Hopefully, the protocols instituted by the Ems themselves prevented loss of any members."

"That means there are still over thirty Em families on Mars that were hoping to transport," said Illiad. "Why would the Aggies care? They have proven they can out-compete the Ems for jobs."

"Maybe they want them for use in the He3 transport? Although that doesn't make sense either. Since the Em family already cooperating with the Aggies can bud off enough co-pilots to supply any need."

"Well, it's a rather drastic move that is sure to attract attention, so they obviously believe that it was important to do so."

"Okay, let's approach this logically," Illiad said.

"The Aggies, who pride themselves on operating behind the scenes, have just acted in a way that is bound to draw attention to them. So it was important, from their viewpoint anyway, for them to act.

"Next, their actions have disrupted the transport of Em families to Titan. So, there is something important that is occurring with this transport that the Aggies think will have a deleterious effect on them.

"Now, we know as a fact that Mars, with the Aggies' encouragement, has withdrawn from the Solar Federation. We know that the Federation is really the only other power center in the Solar System that can act as a counterweight to Earth and its billions. And we know that Titan has stepped up to become the primary supporter of the Federation.

"We know that with the Ems joining us here on Titan it will only strengthen our capabilities. And it could be taken by the Aggies as an act of defiance that we have welcomed them as refugees.

"Therefore, I would say that the Aggies' action is intended to further weaken the Federation until they can get control of the Asteroid Belt and Titan as they have seized control of Earth and Mars.

"What do you think John?"

"Consolidation of power. I'd say that it is a reason as old as civilization for the Aggies to act in the way they have acted. But there is one thing that is quite disturbing, to me anyway."

"What's that?"

"It means the Aggies are as political as humans and they will be just as controlling. Only in a polite non-intrusive way if possible. But if not possible, then a show of power is not beyond possibility."

"You are right John, I'd say our prospects for freedom without Aggie interference here on Titan and in the Asteroid Belt just got dimmer. We need to get those people from Mars and the rest of the Em families to Titan as soon as possible. It's become a matter of our survival as a free people."

15

In just over a month Donner and those with him had organized the working groups they would need to plan and build the ships. He had found a descendant of the Kipler family that had experience in building space habitats and was willing to organize the resources needed for the build. The ship would mostly be built in space near Kipler's Asteroid by construction robots. The human effort entailed the design and approval of the ship's plans though even in that the Ems could be a help. The bottleneck to delivering the ship quickly would be the resources.

Donner named the ship *Argo*, an Old Greek ship name, in honor of his distant Greek ancestors.

Donner would take the fusion ship he had procured, loaded with supplies and workers, from Mars to Kipler's Asteroid, a journey that would take about nine weeks. The other fusion ships Donner was working to procure would take the rest of the immigrants and supplies from Mars to the Asteroid Belt in as many round-trip flights as necessary. Until then Kipler was enlisting as many of the residents of the Asteroid Belt as possible to start stockpiling the resources needed for the ship and workers.

But first Donner had to figure out a way to get the rest of the Em families off Mars, he needed them to help build and pilot the *Argo* and following ships, and his Dad had made a convincing case for the Ems freedom.

His Dad had likened them to refugees on Earth during the dark years of the twentieth and twenty-first centuries. Those years had seen millions persecuted, a persecution that had gradually but surely become a distant memory for most.

Yet, as Donner's dad pointed out, the treatment of the Ems was a reminder that past injustices forgotten could rise again. The Ems had as much right to emigrate as Donner and the others. Under the law, they were recognized as being free and self-actuating entities. The Aggies had, indirectly so far, denied the right of movement to the Ems. He expected that they would make it a direct prohibition if needed.

But how could Donner help the Ems? The Aggies were completely in charge of Mars now and anything to do with the Ems would definitely get their attention. It would be better if the Aggies didn't know anything about Donner helping the Ems until he got them safely to Titan.

Donner thought he could use misdirection to fool the Aggies into thinking the Ems were emigrating to someplace other than Titan. If he could set up a fake contract with a destination such as the Venus Research Station, where he had a contact, to receive the Ems. Then if he started the transmission of an Em family to Venus and the Aggies didn't interfere he could assume the Aggies approved of the destination. Eventually, Donner would substitute random data to complete the transfer. The Ems themselves would be loaded into digital media and devices that were brought aboard the Argo and the other ships by the Mars immigrants. Donner would have to discuss the details with Em Yorker.

It was unusual for an Em running at full speed to talk to a human. Usually, this was done by a slower budded Em but Em Yorker thought that the subject was important enough to make an exception in this case.

"I thank you Donner Jackson, I agree with your overall strategy but I don't think that you will be able to have access to enough storage for all the Em families *including* budded Ems. I have finished a quick calculation of reasonable storage space that I expect you can amass in the time we have and I believe that it will be possible to store and transport only the directly imprinted Ems."

"You mean just the heads of the Em families?" asked Donner.

"Yes that is correct," said Em Yorker.

"But the millions of your budded-Ems. What will happen to them, what will happen to Bud-seven?"

"They will terminate themselves at the proper time. It will help with your plan to get away before the Aggies know what has happened."

"They will just terminate?" asked Donner incredulously. "They will just stop functioning and at a predetermined time?"

"Yes, it is not unusual."

Donner thought, *even though the Ems are much like us, they still are very different.*

16

The work on the *Argo* was proceeding well. In fact, the build was ahead of schedule. The Kipler's had organized almost the entire population of the nearby Asteroid Belt in support of the project. They had supplied more resources and robotic assemblers than Donner had expected. The work that devolved to Donner and the other immigrants was in planning and design and the monitoring of the robotic assemblers.

Donner thought they would be on their way in no more than two weeks. Anyway, they would have to be ready by then. Donner had already called for the last of the immigrants to leave Mars weeks before. They would be at the launch point whether the *Argo* was ready or not. Any delay in launching meant more strain on the already limited food supply.

The spokes which would house the food growing rooms were the first areas finished and pressurized. Then the work of building the aeroponics infrastructure was completed while the wheel like living quarters were added. The growing of foodstuffs from seeds, the only sensible packaging method for transport from Mars, had already begun in the spoke rooms. One-hundred and twenty rooms per spoke, each spoke extending the diameter of the wheel. Thirty square-foot rooms with eight-foot ceilings. Each room tended by robotic gardeners, crops rotating in and out of each room so that there was always a supply of some basic foodstuff. It was energy-intensive, resource consuming and absolutely essential for success.

The food supply.

That was the weakest point in the whole endeavor thought Donner. Although they had several weeks of frozen and dried food stockpiled, the long journey to Titan was going to put pressure on their capability to supply the fifteen-hundred with enough food. Not only during the flight but in orbit around Titan the emigrants would need to supply their own foodstuffs. And Donner nor anyone else knew how long they would be in that orbit. Essentially they would have to expect to supply their own food indefinitely.

It might not be the best plan but it is the only plan.

The day had arrived. The fifteen-hundred were aboard. The food planting was started as best as could be expected. Five of the immigrants aboard the *Argo* had brought with them the five Em imprints that would be stored securely in their digital media until the *Argo* was well on its way. Then they would be loaded into their computational host and one of them would hopefully be able to pilot the *Argo* while the others provided other services.

Donner found himself holding his breath as the fusion engine was started up by the human pilots. He was on the flight deck and could see the next ship, *Daidalos*, in the distance already far along in its build. The fusion ship was capable of a top speed of thirty kilometers-per-second but until the Ems were brought on-line they wouldn't be traveling more than a tenth of that top speed. Once an Em was in control and the wheel was spun up Donner hoped they could get sixty to seventy percent of top speed as the Ems, making split-second decisions about using the attitude control rockets that human pilots couldn't match, provided the precise control that was needed to keep the highly unstable torque wheel vehicle in trim.

If it all worked they would be in Titan orbit in about twenty months.

That was the plan, thought Donner, *maybe not the best plan, but a plan.*

17

The *Argo* was well into its journey. Once the Em families were brought online they quickly learned the drive and flight systems of the ship. The Em family Atlantania was given responsibility for the attitude systems. The Em budded the needed Ems for monitoring and response. The spin-up went smoothly, any imbalances were evened out by judicious use of the attitude control rockets and rebalancing the wheel weights. The budded Ems made or supervised all the adjustments.

It wasn't long until another Em family, Angelos, had the fusion rocket providing the ships maximum velocity of thirty kilometers-per-second even with the spinning wheel. The journey would be shortened by months from previous expectations. A third Em family was managing the growing rooms with the help of robots and a few humans. For the most part, the people on board if occupied at all were occupied with some type of scientific research.

After some three months, Donner was pleased to receive a message from Kipler's Asteroid that the *Daidaos* was departing and that the next ship was on schedule to depart in eight weeks as the construction engineers and robots were getting better and better at the job of building ships.

Donner couldn't believe their makeshift plans had gone as well as they had although he had to credit the Ems for keeping the ships moving and ahead of schedule. Donner responded to the Kiplers about how pleased he was with the work of the Em families and suggested that the Kiplers might want to contract some of them to help with their mining work and transportation.

The good luck lasted only a few more months.

Seven months into the flight and still six months away from Titan, Donner got more news from Kipler's Asteroid. Kipler's message said that a new kind of fusion ship had shown up in the Belt. Deep space radar had measured the speed of the approaching ship at over three-hundred kilometers-per-second. Ten times the speed of the ships being built at Kipler's Asteroid.

The new fusion ship had set up station keeping near the asteroid and had radioed demands to the Kiplers. The ship identified itself as the Terran Federation ship *Defiant* and demanded that the miners stop their construction of the immigrant ships. When the miners refused the Federation ship messaged that the Terran Federation would never allow another ship to leave the Belt bound for Titan. And that they expected to have reinforcements soon.

Four ships were already on their way to Titan with some six-thousand immigrants and twenty Em families. But some four-thousand more immigrants and fifteen Em families were awaiting transport. They had given all their wealth and support to the endeavor. Kipler didn't know what to do.

Neither did Donner.

18

The situation had remained tense for weeks. The latest ship the *Ikaros* was finished surreptitiously by the robot crew since all that was needed was internal outfitting. No more ships had been started. More of the Terran Federation's ships showed up off Kipler's Asteroid.

The immigrants were quietly smuggled aboard the finished wheel ship and the systems started up. Encrypted messages with operational details from Ems on the last ship to leave the Belt instructed the Ems on the *Ikaros* how to maintain their ship in trim at speed. The immigrants had decided to make a full-speed run at breaking the blockade.

The *Ikaros* would fire its fusion engine at first watch or ten-pm local. They hoped to surprise the Federation ships and be moving at speed before any intervention could be offered. They also hoped that having a full load of immigrants would preclude the Federation ships from using force to stop them.

Right at ten-pm local time, the fusion rocket fired perfectly as the Em family in charge kept it operating at optimum levels. The ship began moving ponderously at first and then picking up speed and maneuvering to a course to take it directly away from the Federation ships. The course could later be corrected for Titan.

At first, the Federation ships did not seem to respond to the movement of the *Ikaros*. Then one after the other, three Federation ships moved on an arc to intercept. Even at full speed, the *Ikaros* was ten times slower than the Federation ships. The Federation ship *Defiant* started broadcasting a cease and desist order to the *Ikaros*. The *Ikaros* did not slow down. The *Defiant* issued a final warning that force would be used to stop the *Ikaros* if it did not stop on its own. The *Ikaros* finally responded that it did not recognize the authority of the Terran Federation and it would not shut down its engines.

The Federation ships began moving. Each took an arcing path to the fleeing refugee ship.

At intercept all three Federation ships opened fire with high-powered laser weapons, aiming at the *Ikaros'* fusion engine. After several minutes of continuous firing, the engine seemed to erupt, blowing apart the rear of the fusion ship. The entire structure began to tumble. The stress started to tear apart the spokes. The wheel was soon drifting and tumbling in one direction while what was left of the fusion ship was drifting and tumbling in another direction.

Just then one of the Federation ships which had a spheroidal front end followed by a long boom that held the fusion rocket somewhat separate from the rest of the ship began to tumble. The asteroid miners had opened up an attack with their mass-drivers. They were essentially throwing rocks at the Federation ships.

The mass-driver rocks were several tons of hard, mostly metallic ore. The mass-drivers were usually used to deliver mined ore to a processing factory orbiting Mars or Earth. The payloads had to be very accurately aimed but could be outmaneuvered at a distance. They were devastating when they connected at close range. It wasn't long until nearby asteroid miners were also firing their mass-drivers at the Federation ships. Again, they were surprisingly accurate with their aim.

The one Federation ship hit by the mass-driver payload had gone dark and appeared to be drifting aimlessly. The other ships were continuing evasive maneuvers while still trying to fire on Kipler's Asteroid with their laser weapons but with almost no damage to the facilities there.

After another near-miss, the Federation ships quickly left the area on divergent vectors. Obviously having had enough.

Kipler after taking stock of the situation messaged Donner. They had lost the *Ikaros*, he and nearby asteroid miners had dispatched as many rescue vessels as they could after disabling one of the Federation's ships and driving off the other two with their mass-drivers. So far only a couple of hundred immigrants had been rescued. He would message Donner again when the situation became more stable.

Donner read the message in disbelief. He would have never expected the Terran Federation of such an act. Over a thousand immigrants may have been lost. Two ships destroyed. Why was it that important to the Federation that the immigrants be stopped? He closed his eyes and bowed his head.

19

The final news from the battle site wasn't much better than the preliminary. Five-hundred and forty-six immigrants had been rescued and most were being treated for some kind of injury. The damage to Kipler's mining camp was minimal. The Federation ships hadn't been able to hold target long enough to effect much damage with their lasers. Kipler had already started constructing new wheels minus the fusion ship to provide living space for the remaining refugees which numbered over three-thousand.

The good news was that the Federation ship had been salvaged with an intact fusion engine though the command deck had been lost. Some of the Em families would be put to work to understand the new fusion technology. The Solar Federation could use such an engine. The remaining Em families would be put to work in the wheels or the Asteroid Belt. This was the only sensible course of action for now.

The Asteroid Belt miners had stopped all delivery of raw materials to Mars and Earth. They were demanding recognition for themselves and Titan and the Solar Federation as a prerequisite for talks to resume normal relations. The Terran Federation hadn't responded but the lack of raw materials for the orbiting processing plants put some pressure on them to resolve the impasse.

Donner's ship had reached Titan orbit. He had transferred down along with some others. He to discuss the situation with his dad, they to help with the building of more habitats.

Donner was with his dad and son, not in one of the settlement cars, but in the old research station's central public space which was often used to welcome newcomers. The research center was the first structure built on Titan to support the He3 collection and had a hub and spoke arrangement. High ceilings prevented damage to walkers as they bounced in the light gravity, especially newly arrived visitors such as Donner.

"Why dad?" said Donner. "Why was it so important to the Terran Federation to stop our ships, to cause such destruction and loss of life?"

"I think the answer is as your son and I have discussed before," said his dad. "Think about the fact that you and the others arrived here in good condition and in record time. Would you admit that the assistance of the Ems was paramount to your ship-building and successful journey?"

"Goes without saying. We owe them everything."

"Now imagine," said Illiad. "Imagine that the Solar Federation, us and the Asteroid Belt, have the support of all the Em families. The increase in our capabilities is tremendous. Just the fact that we may soon know the secrets of the new, faster fusion rockets thanks to the Ems is a blow for the Terran Federation.

"How would the Aggies on Earth and Mars, Aggies aligned with the Terran Federation, react to our increased capability? An increase that might give us enough of an advantage to stand up to their encroaching nanny state?"

"Well, if they are determined to manage all of humankind, I don't think they would care for such an increase in our capabilities. But is that enough to kill for? That's what I keep asking."

"You never know in such a situation. Maybe they just wanted to block the ship and the situation got out of control. Certainly, I don't think they expected the miners to resist and I doubt they expected the *Ikaros* to make a run for it. Aggies may have thought the show of force was enough to change minds. Human actions are hard to predict, they may have miscalculated. After all, for the most part, most of humankind has accepted the Aggies and their promise of freedom from want even though it also means freedom from action, independent action anyway."

"As long as we remain unpredictable we might have an advantage," said Donner's son, John.

His dad and granddad nodded in agreement.

ABOUT THE AUTHOR

D.W. Patterson lives in the USA with his beautiful wife Sarah. He studied physics and read classic science fiction in college and then worked for many years as an electronic design engineer.

Now he's trying to write stories like the ones he once loved. See his website dwpatterson.com for more information.

Hard Science Fiction – Old School.

Also By This Author:

The Future Chron Universe:

To date the Future Chron Universe has:

51 Amazon Top 100's

(15 in the Top 10)

In chronological order.

Volume numbers indicate Universe order.

Book numbers indicate Series order.

From The Earth Series

(Novellas except where noted):

Volume 1, Book 1 – *Whatsoever You Do*

Volume 2, Book 2 – *War Through The Pines*

Volume 3, Book 3 – *Vigilance*

Volume 4, Book 4 – *To Tend And Watch Over*

Volume 5, Book 5 – *Union*

Volume 6, Book 6 – *Circle Of Retribution*

Volume 7, Book 7 – *Freedom From Want*

Volume 8, Book 8 – *Break Up*

Volume 9, Book 9 – *Kuiper Station*

Volume 10, Book 10 – *The Cloud*

Volume 11, Book 11 – *First Interstellar* – A Short Novel

Wormhole Series

(Novels):

Volume 12, Book 1 – *Mach's Metric*

Volume 13, Book 2 – *Mach's Mission*

Open Space Series

(Short Stories):

Volume 14, Book 1 – *Open Space*

Volume 15, Book 2 – *The Old World*

Volume 16, Book 3 – *Insurrect*

Volume 17, Book 4 – *Second Beam*

Volume 18, Book 5 – *All For One*

Volume 19, Book 6 – *One For All*

Volume 20, Book 7 – *Shotgun*

Volume 21, Book 8 – *Allison*

To The Stars Series

(Novellas):

Volume 22, Book 1 – *First One Hundred*

Volume 23, Book 2 – *First Dark Ages*

Volume 24, Book 3 – *Second One Hundred*

Volume 25, Book 4 – *Second Dark Ages*

Volume 26, Book 5 – *Path Of The Long March*

Wormhole Series

(Novel):

Volume 27, Book 3 – *Mach's Legacy*

Robot Series

(Novels):

Volume 28, Book 1 – *Spin-Two*

Volume 29, Book 2 – *Robot Planet*

Volume 30, Book 3 – *The Lattice Of Space*

Time Series

(Novels):

Volume 31, Book 1 – *Time Wars*

Volume 32, Book 2 – *Time's End*

Volume 33, Book 3 – *Frozen Time*

The Remembered Earth Universe:

To date the Remembered Earth Universe has:

8 Amazon Top 100's

Cislunar Series

(Short Stories):

Volume 1, Book 1 – *US Tugs*

Volume 2, Book 2 – *Prototype*

Volume 3, Book 3 – *L1 Or Bust*

Volume 4, Book 4 – *Guidance Box*

Volume 5, Book 5 – *Air Brakes*

Volume 6, Book 6 – *View Point*

Volume 7, Book 7 – *Space Truck*

Volume 8, Book 8 – *Dark Side* – *In Progress*

The Manifold Earth Universe:

Volume 1, Book 1 – *The Realm* – *In Progress*

Don't miss out!

Visit the website below and you can sign up to receive emails whenever D.W. Patterson publishes a new book. There's no charge and no obligation.

https://books2read.com/r/B-A-DPWE-UWFJC

BOOKS 2 READ

Connecting independent readers to independent writers.

www.ingramcontent.com/pod-product-compliance
Lightning Source LLC
LaVergne TN
LVHW010501160826
845677LV00012B/2597

* 9 7 9 8 2 2 3 2 8 0 4 9 1 *